AHYOKA
and the Talking Leaves

BY PETER AND CONNIE ROOP
ILLUSTRATIONS BY YOSHI MIYAKE

A Beech Tree Paperback Book
New York

FOR HEIDI,
our Ahyoka, who brings us much happiness.

The authors wish to express appreciation and gratitude to Kevin W. Smith, Curatorial Assistant of the Native American Collections at the Philbrook Museum of Art, Tulsa, Oklahoma, and Consultant to the Cherokee Heritage Center in Tahlequah, for sharing his expertise and knowledge of the Cherokee people and language.

First Beech Tree Edition, 1994.
1 3 5 7 9 10 8 6 4 2

Library of Congress Cataloging in Publication Data
Roop, Peter. Ahyoka and the talking leaves/by Peter and Connie Roop; illustrated by Yoshi Miyake.
p. cm.   Summary: Ahyoka helps her father Sequoyah in his quest to create a system of writing for his people.   ISBN 0-688-13082-8   1. Sequoya, 1770?–1843—Juvenile fiction. 2. Cherokee Indians—Juvenile fiction. [1. Sequoya, 1770?–1843—Fiction. 2. Cherokee Indians—Fiction. 3. Indians of North America—Fiction. 4. Writing—Fiction. 5. Fathers and daughters—Fiction.] I. Roop, Connie. II. Miyake, Yoshi, ill. III. Title.   PZ7.R6723Ah 1992
[Fic]—dc20   91-30366   CIP AC

THE CHEROKEE SYLLABARY

D a			R e			
S ga	Ꮨ ka		Ꮆ ge			
Ꮬ ha			Ꮅ he			
W la			Ꮈ le			
Ꮏ ma			Ꮊ me			
Ꮎ na	Ꮏ hna	Ꮹ nah	Ꮑ ne			
Ꮖ qua			Ꮗ que			
Ꮋ sa	Ꮝ s		Ꮞ se			
Ꮮ da	Ꮃ ta		Ꮥ de	Ꮦ te		
Ꮪ dla	Ꮣ tla		Ꮧ tle			
Ꮳ tsa			Ꮴ tse			
Ꮹ wa			Ꮺ we			
Ꮿ ya			Ꮙ ye			

T i	Ꮴ o	Ꭴ u	i v
Ꭹ gi	A go	J gu	E gv
Ꭿ hi	Ꭶ ho	Ꭽ hu	Ꮂ hv
Ꮅ li	Ꮑ lo	M lu	Ꮙ lv
H mi	Ꮠ mo	Ꭹ mu	
Ꮒ ni	Z no	Ꮔ nu	Ꮟ nv
Ꮚ qui	Ꮼ quo	Ꮖ quu	Ꮛ quv
Ꮍ si	Ꮺ so	Ꮡ su	R sv
Ꮧ di	Ꮨ ti	V do	Ꮪ du	Ꮫ dv
C tli	Ꮯ tlo	Ꮰ tlu	P tlv
Ꮵ tsi	K tso	Ꮳ tsu	Ꮶ tsv
Ꮻ wi	Ꮼ wo	Ꮗ wu	Ꮾ wv
Ꮙ yi	Ꮿ yo	Ꮍ yu	B yv

D Ꭶ Ꮙ   ah-yo-ka   Ꮞ Ꮪ Ꮿ   se-quo-ya

ONE

Ahyoka's charcoal flew across the sycamore bark.

Would Father understand her picture? Sometimes he knew what her drawings meant. Other times he did not. When she had drawn her best buffalo, he had thought it was a cow.

For two summers and two winters Ahyoka and her father, Sequoyah, had been drawing pictures for the Tsalagi people's words. The Cherokee had so many words, and she and Sequoyah had to draw a picture for every one of them. The stack of drawings in the corner reached Ahyoka's chin. Yet she felt as if they had just begun.

There were still so many more words to draw: Gadu, bread. Ahawi, deer. Waya, wolf. And those were the easy words. What would she draw for hard ones, for anger, sorrow, dusk, autumn?

Ahyoka sighed. Even if they drew every Cherokee word, would her people understand them? How could they learn to read all those pictures? Even she had trouble remembering them. And yet, white men had done it. They could read their words on the talking leaves.

Suddenly Ahyoka's mother yanked the picture off her lap.

"You are supposed to be stitching moccasins. But here you are again, making pictures . . . talking leaves! What good are they? They don't make moccasins to trade. They don't feed the chickens or plant corn or . . ."

She stared at the fire for a moment, then flung Ahyoka's picture into the flames.

"Mother!" cried Ahyoka. She grabbed the picture and brushed it off. Soot and charcoal smudged her deerskin dress.

"Once, we had a good farm," Utiya

snapped. "Once, your father made the best silver jewelry in the Cherokee Nation. People came from miles away to buy his silver."

Ahyoka caressed her silver bracelet. Two years earlier, Sequoyah had made it to celebrate her sixth season of life. He had not worked silver since.

"Now no one comes to our door," Utiya continued, "except to ask for payment of our debts. Day and night your father thinks only of talking leaves. And you are becoming just as bad! I need you to make moccasins, not talking leaves. Someday I am going to burn that whole stack!"

Mother was right. Father thought only of talking leaves. He wanted to help his people. He wanted the Tsalagi to read and write. He wanted them to understand the treaties they signed so that the white men could no longer steal their land. Why couldn't Mother understand?

Utiya bundled up the last of the snakeroot that they had gathered the spring before. She shoved it at Ahyoka. Ahyoka dropped her picture to take it.

"We have nothing else left to trade," Utiya said. "Now go find your father. I need four needles from the trader in the village. And tell him to get red thread from your aunt Tsiya so that we can finish these moccasins."

Ahyoka picked up her drawing and started down the trail. Her mother's words chased after her.

"And don't waste time on those useless talking leaves!"

TWO

Silent as a chipmunk, Ahyoka slipped along the path. She knew exactly where to find her father. A huge hickory tree stood deep in the forest. Sequoyah often went there when he wanted to be alone. Since winter had ended, he went there every day.

Ahyoka hid behind a tree. Perhaps she could surprise her father. He sat against the hickory, his walking stick beside him on the ground. He held his hands out, then slowly turned them. Ahyoka saw the light dance over his palms. He picked up a wedge of charcoal and began to draw.

6

He must be drawing agaliha, sunshine, Ahyoka thought. A difficult word-picture, almost as difficult as anger. She had never seen Utiya as angry as she'd been that morning. It was as though something had snapped inside her. How could Ahyoka ever draw such fury? Just then her foot slipped, breaking a dry, thin branch. That was it! A broken stick could mean anger!

At the sound, Sequoyah raised his head. Ahyoka stepped from behind the tree.

"Hold out your hands," he told her. Light filled Ahyoka's hands and flashed from her bracelet. "See how the sunshine dances. How can we ever draw the words to say that?" His shoulders slumped.

As Ahyoka sat down beside her father, a squirrel scurried past. Overhead, a woodpecker tapped for insects. Sequoyah's charcoal scraped across the bark as he tried to draw the dancing sunlight.

At last he laid his charcoal down. "What new word have you drawn?" he asked.

Ahyoka handed him her picture. He

turned it one way, then another. He pulled it close to his eyes. He held it at arm's length.

"Are these our Big Mountains?"

"No, Father," Ahyoka said. "We already drew that."

"Then it must be the mounds in which we plant corn in the spring."

Ahyoka shook her head. Could he really not tell, or was he teasing her?

Sequoyah laughed and looked into her eyes. "It is our stream," he told her.

Ahyoka laughed too. He had known it all the time.

"How did it get smeared?" Sequoyah asked.

Ahyoka had forgotten all about the smudge marks. She had forgotten why she was there.

"Mother needs needles and thread." Ahyoka's words spilled out. "She is very angry this time. She threw my picture into the fire. We must go to the village right now!"

"Your mother has been angry before," Sequoyah answered calmly. "No doubt, she will be angry again." He picked up his

9

walking stick. "Come on, you broken twig," he said, rubbing his lame leg. "A walk will feel good after all this sitting."

They set off down the mountain to Willstown.

"Tell me again how you learned of the talking leaves," Ahyoka begged.

"Again?" Sequoyah asked. "You have heard that story many times."

"Then I will hear it one more time. Please."

"Ahyoka, you are as persistent as a mosquito. You will pester me until I tell you."

"That will be the next picture I draw," she said. "Dosaudvna bothering a big man. It will mean pester." Sequoyah chuckled.

"When you were just a newborn baby," he began, "I was a soldier in the American Army. We were fighting the Creeks, far away at Horseshoe Bend. How I missed your mother and brothers! I wondered how tall the corn grew. I worried whether my family was hungry. Most of all, I wanted to know about you, Ahyoka, whom we named She

Who Brought Happiness. I was lonely and missed the happiness that you brought us.

"The white soldiers looked at leaves of paper sent by their families. The marks on the papers spoke to them. They told how tall the corn was at home. They told whether the hunting was good or bad. They told when someone was sick or when a baby was born or when someone died.

"Why couldn't we, the Real People, have talking leaves, I asked myself. Then I would know about my family. Utiya would know about me. Real People everywhere would know what happened to loved ones far away. I decided then that no matter how long it took, I would make talking leaves for our people!"

They stopped to rest at an abandoned cabin. While Sequoyah leaned on his cane and filled his clay pipe, Ahyoka peered through the door into the gloomy darkness.

"Why did Climbing Bear and his family move away?" she asked.

Sequoyah stared at the cabin. He puffed

his pipe, and small clouds of smoke rose above his head. At last he spoke. "They loved the old ways of the Real People. They did not like the new things that were happening. They said the Tsalagi were becoming too much like the white man: fighting his wars, building churches, farming with plows. They wanted to go back to the days before the white men came. We have heard nothing of them for three winters now."

"If we had talking leaves, we could write to them," Ahyoka said.

"*If* we had talking leaves," Sequoyah repeated sadly. He tapped his pipe out. "Come, Ahyoka. We have rested long enough. Perhaps Mr. Adair found a book of talking leaves for us. I would like you to see it," Sequoyah said.

"Is the secret of the talking leaves in a book, Father?" Ahyoka asked.

"I don't know, my daughter. Once, when I visited a mission school, I saw boys and girls your age learning from books."

"Then why can't we learn from their books?"

"Books speak English. We want leaves that talk the words of our people."

When will we have them? wondered Ahyoka as they followed the trail down the mountain.

THREE

An hour later, they stopped at the Etowah River. The square log cabins and hump-backed lodges of Willstown stood on the west bank. Ahyoka and Sequoyah crossed the shallow ford. Near the Council House, naked boys chased one another. Girls pounded corn while grandmothers spun cotton thread. Ahyoka and Sequoyah stepped over dogs plopped in the dust.

They found Mr. Adair, the trader, in front of the Council House. Ahyoka liked Mr. Adair. He was always so friendly to them. His wares were spread out on a large gray blanket. Her eyes skimmed over the buttons, beads, fishhooks, ax heads, steel knives, pots, and skillets. She saw nothing that might be a book.

"I was hoping you two would come to town while I was trading. You look as pretty as a sunflower in full bloom, Ahyoka," Mr. Adair said in greeting. "But I wish you were still making jewelry, Sequoyah. From the Tennessee River to the Chattahoochee, people keep asking for Sequoyah's silver. I could trade a packful!"

"I have not had time for working silver," Sequoyah replied. "I am working on the talking leaves."

"And I am helping him," Ahyoka added.

"Well, I guess I am helping too. It took a lot of looking, but I finally found a book for you." Mr. Adair reached into his pack and Ahyoka's eyes brightened. He pulled out a thin leather-covered book and handed it to Sequoyah.

Sequoyah held the book as tenderly as a baby bird. Ahyoka longed to reach out and touch it. She and Sequoyah stood gazing at the book. Then, without opening it, Sequoyah handed it to her.

Ahyoka stroked the leather cover. It was as soft as her mother's best moccasins. A golden tree, as smooth and cool as her bracelet, spread its branches across the crinkled leather. Then she opened it. Tiny black marks marched across the white pages.

Ahyoka pointed to the black lines. "Are these the marks that speak?" she asked.

"Yes," answered Mr. Adair. "This is a spelling book. The marks tell how to write words."

"But how can they talk, Father?" asked Ahyoka.

"That is the secret," Sequoyah answered. "These leaves talk English. We must make them speak Tsalagi."

"Can you make the marks speak, Mr. Adair?" Ahyoka asked.

"No. They don't make any sense to me. I can't read them either."

"Thank you for bringing the book," Sequoyah said. "I have Utiya's best snakeroot to trade for it."

Ahyoka held her breath. What would Mother say when she found out they traded her snakeroot for a book?

Mr. Adair frowned and shook his head. "I need more than snakeroot for the book, Sequoyah! Books are as rare as wings on bears around here. I did some hard trading to get this for you," he said.

Ahyoka ran her fingers over the leather cover again. Mr. Adair held out his palm. Reluctantly, she handed him the book. She could hardly bear to look at her father. His eyes seemed like those of a dying doe.

"I hope I find someone else who wants it," Mr. Adair grumbled, shoving the book back into his pack. "I ain't got no use for it."

The three stood in silence. Ahyoka rubbed her silver bracelet.

"We must go to Tsiya's," Sequoyah said at last.

"You go, Father," Ahyoka told him. "I will get Mother's needles and meet you at the river."

Sequoyah nodded. "Thank you, Mr. Adair, for finding the book," he said. "Another time I will have enough to trade for it." Then he turned away. Ahyoka watched him limp to her aunt's home. She touched her bracelet again. Slowly, she slid the bracelet off her wrist.

"Will you trade the book for my bracelet?" she asked, holding it out. "My father made it."

Mr. Adair took the bracelet. He bounced it in his hand to test the weight of the silver. When his fingers found Sequoyah's mark, he smiled.

"This is the finest piece of Sequoyah's silver I have ever seen. Yes, Ahyoka, I will trade the book for the bracelet. And I will add the needles your mother wants."

The trader opened a small paper packet. Six steel sewing needles flashed in the sunlight.

"These are my best," he said. "Made in England. Utiya will like them."

"Not when she finds out I traded my bracelet for a book." Ahyoka sighed. "But I still have the snakeroot. And two extra needles. That should help to please her."

Mr. Adair handed the book to Ahyoka. She traced the shapes on the cover, running her fingers up and down the trunk of the golden tree. Then she carefully put the book into her pouch and looked at Mr. Adair. "If my father comes back, do not tell him about our trade. I do not know if he will be pleased. And I want to surprise him."

Mr. Adair shook his head. "I sure don't understand why he wants to learn how to read so bad. I've never seen a man so set upon something."

Why doesn't anyone want talking leaves as Father does? wondered Ahyoka as she flew from the village. She hoped Sequoyah would be waiting for her by the river. She could hardly wait to see his look of surprise when she handed him the book. Then she thought again. He might make her return it. She should be patient and show him after they left Willstown.

Sequoyah was not at the ford, so Ahyoka opened the book and puzzled over the marks. There were circle shapes like the sun, smaller moon circles, dots like young stars. There were lines like arrow shafts, snake shapes, shapes like mountains. But none of the shapes made sense to her. When she looked at one of her father's drawings, she knew what animal or plant it was. Bird tracks in mud told which way the bird was going and what kind it was. But Ahyoka could not fathom the meaning of a snail crawling up a reed beside the full moon. The word "do" appeared too often to make any sense at all to Ahyoka.

Ahyoka shook her head and looked up. Her father was coming! Quickly, she slipped the book back into her pouch and carefully squeezed the snakeroot in with it.

"Look, Father," she called, running to meet him. "Six needles for Mother! I know she will be pleased." She hoped he would not see that her bracelet was gone or that her pouch was full.

"At least you made a good trade, Ahyoka," he said. "And I have the thread. We must return home now."

They traveled without talking. The late-afternoon sun warmed their backs. Once, a black snake slithered to cover as they neared. Blue jays squawked at them. Insects hummed.

The book bounced against Ahyoka's hip as she walked. She patted the pouch, hoping the solution to the mystery of the talking leaves was in it. Several times, she reached for the book to show Sequoyah but decided to wait until they stopped to rest. She felt as though she was going to pop like dried corn thrown into a crackling fire.

At last she saw Climbing Bear's abandoned cabin. "My feet are tired. Let's stop, Father," she suggested.

"Only for as long as it takes a squirrel to crack a nut," Sequoyah answered. "Your mother will be angry enough with us as it is."

Without looking at her father, Ahyoka slowly opened her pouch and touched the book. The leather felt cool. She ran her hand down the crinkled spine. "Father, I traded my bracelet for the book."

Sequoyah took a deep breath. Then he

let it out in a long sigh. He stared at his daughter.

"Father, please don't be angry," Ahyoka pleaded. "Don't make me take it back. I want you to have it." She placed the book in her father's hands.

Sequoyah opened the cover. "Ahyoka. She Who Brought Happiness," he said. "Your heart truly does believe in the talking leaves." He ran his fingers over the pages. "I hope Adanvdo, the Great Spirit, will open our eyes to its mystery."

They talked as they walked. What did the suns and arrows on the pages mean? They were not pictures, yet they spoke to the white people. How could they be made to speak to the Real People?

Soon their cabin was in sight. Gray smoke rose from its chimney.

"Smell that, Ahyoka?" said Sequoyah. "Mother must be roasting squirrel for dinner."

"Did you shoot a squirrel?" Ahyoka asked.

"No," he answered, suddenly puzzled.

All at once Ahyoka understood. "Our pictures!" she shouted. "Mother is burning our pictures!"

Ahyoka raced to the cabin. She flung open the door. The stack of pictures was gone! Utiya was throwing the last one into the flames. Ahyoka burst into tears.

"I warned you," Utiya shouted. "I said I would burn them!"

Sequoyah stood in the cabin doorway, staring. His fingers gripped his walking stick like the claws of an owl. Sparks shot up the chimney as he turned to face Utiya. Ahyoka had never seen anyone so angry.

"I will live here no longer," Sequoyah thundered.

"No, Father," Ahyoka cried, rushing to his side. "You cannot leave us."

He knelt and pulled her close. She felt the strength of his arms. "I must go, Ahyoka. This is no home for me." Ahyoka trembled as she buried her face in his chest, her tears staining his shirt. She sensed his heart's sadness.

"I will go with you," she cried.

"Stay," he whispered. Ahyoka thought she heard tears in his voice. "Your mother needs you."

"You need me too," said Ahyoka. "I can help you draw the pictures again."

"No," Sequoyah said. "I must walk this trail alone."

Ahyoka watched her father put the book into a patched cooking pot and cover it with a blanket. Then, clasping his walking stick in one hand and the pot in the other, he limped out the door.

How could I ever draw the way I feel now? wondered Ahyoka as Utiya shut the door.

FOUR

That evening Ahyoka milked the cow. She carried in firewood. She swept the dirt floor. She wondered where her father was.

"Come, Ahyoka, sit with me by the fire," her mother urged. "We will be better off without him."

"Why?" Ahyoka cried.

"Because talking leaves don't fill empty stomachs. Your father is gone. I need you to do needlework on the moccasins we can sell. I need you to help me collect snakeroot and other plants to trade."

Ahyoka said nothing.

She cried as she climbed into bed. She

hugged her doll tight, but she did not sleep for a long time. Was she going to stay with her mother or join her father?

It was still dark when Ahyoka awoke and crept out of bed. Shivering, she pulled her blanket around her shoulders. Was Father cold too? She went to the window. The stars flickered like faraway campfires. The moon hung from a pine branch. Ugugu, the owl, swooped past on silent wings. She heard talasgewi squeal. Then ugugu rose, the mouse dangling from its claws.

She put a flint and steel for starting fires into her leather pouch, along with needle and thread and a sharp knife. She wrapped a second blanket over her shoulders. In her arm she cradled the cornhusk doll her mother had made for her.

Ahyoka looked at her sleeping mother.

"Good-bye," she whispered. "I will miss you. Someday I will come back. Maybe then you will understand us." She quietly opened the door and stepped into the darkness.

There was a bundle by the door—her father's clothes! She knew now that he would never return. By putting Sequoyah's clothes outside, her mother had divorced him. Ahyoka picked up the bundle.

Where was he? Had he gone to the village? She would look there first.

Ahyoka had never walked alone to the village at night. She stood rigid at the edge of the clearing. The woods were so dark. Trees she loved to climb loomed like the monsters in her grandmother's stories. She turned back toward the cabin and took a step. Then she stopped. Would her father have turned back? No! A sudden splash made her jump, but it was only gvli, the raccoon, catching his supper in the creek.

Ahyoka reached for her bracelet to feel its smooth, familiar comfort. But it was gone! She had forgotten about her trade. Now she recalled the feel of the book's soft leather. She ached to see it again, to hold it, to riffle its pages and look at it with her father. Clutching the bundle and her doll, Ahyoka started down the trail through the forest.

Dark turned slowly to dawn. Birds chirped and called. Mist rose from the creek like the ghosts of the ancient ones. Once, she startled a doe and a fawn. Leaping across the creek, the deer flashed their white tails at her. They would make a good picture for "swift." Her father would be pleased.

In the growing light, Climbing Bear's abandoned cabin looked like an empty hickory shell, cracked and ruined. Was it only yesterday that she had sat there and given Sequoyah the book? How could so much have changed in such a short time?

One by one the campfires faded from the sky until only a single star was left. Then it too disappeared as the sun rolled over a mountaintop and lit the world. Ahyoka smiled at tgaehinvdo, the sun. His light gave her courage. She would find her father. She knew it.

Near Willstown, Ahyoka stopped. She hid her belongings under a rhododendron bush. Then she crossed the river and entered the village.

Willstown was just waking. Small boys

were adding sticks to the cooking fires. Tsiya and five other women were grinding corn-meal for breakfast. Older girls were filling pots and kettles with water from the river. A group of sleepy-eyed little girls were playing with their cornhusk dolls. She could hear the laughter of the older boys and men bathing downstream.

"Good morning, my Grandmothers," Ahyoka said to the women.

Tsiya looked surprised. "Why, Ahyoka," she said, "what brings you back today? Does Utiya need more thread already?"

"I am looking for my father," Ahyoka told her. "Have you seen him? He left us last night."

"Good," said Tsiya. "I have not seen him and I do not want to. I don't understand why Utiya put up with him so long. He has forgotten his family. He has forsaken the duties of a man. It is better he is gone."

"No," Ahyoka cried. "You don't understand, either!" She ran from her aunt.

"Ahyoka, stop," Aunt Tsiya called, but

Ahyoka kept running. She rounded the Council House and crashed into Mr. Adair.

"Ahyoka," he said, laughing. "Is a bear chasing you?"

Ahyoka looked into his eyes. Maybe he would understand. Her breath came in gasps as she told her story.

"Would he be in the Council House?" Mr. Adair suggested.

Ahyoka's heart skipped a beat. Maybe he was. She ran to the door and looked in, but her father was not there. Ahyoka took a deep breath. Then she ran to the river, splashed across, and raced up the trail. She stopped at the bush to get her belongings. A blanket of shade spread beneath it. Suddenly Ahyoka felt so tired that she crawled into the shade and quickly fell asleep.

The sun was halfway past its peak when Ahyoka woke. She did not know where she was. As she sat up, she stuck her head into a spider's web. She brushed the web from her hair and remembered.

Sequoyah! Where was her father? Had he

left the Big Mountains? What should she do? It was a long way home, and the light would soon begin to fade. She did not want to spend the night alone in darkness.

Ahyoka had no choice. She had to return home. Tomorrow she would search again.

The trail up the mountain had never seemed so long. Her legs and arms ached. Her head ached. Twice she filled her empty stomach with long drinks from the creek. She bit a persimmon and spit it out. Another moon must pass before the persimmons, huckleberries, and blackberries would be sweet.

Around a bend in the trail she saw Climbing Bear's cabin. At first she did not see Sequoyah. Shadows hid him. She might have missed him if his hand had not been skimming over a piece of bark.

Ahyoka grabbed the hem of her skirt and ran.

"Father," she called.

Sequoyah looked up from his drawing. "Ahyoka!"

Ahyoka ran to Sequoyah and clung to him like a grapevine. He closed his arms around her.

"I had to find you, Father," she explained. "I could not let you leave forever. I know that together we can make the talking leaves."

"My little mosquito," Sequoyah whispered. "You are as persistent as ever. In my dreams last night, we solved the mystery. Adanvdo looks kindly upon us."

FIVE

Ahyoka and Sequoyah made the cabin their home. They patched the holes in the roof. They hung a blanket for a door. They gathered roots and berries. They talked, and laughed, and sang. They puzzled over the book for hours.

But the marks still made no sense. Even the pages that had pictures did not help. They copied the pictures on bark, but that gave them no clues. The marks remained nothing but lines and circles.

"Each mark must stand for a picture," Sequoyah said one day. "By putting the marks together, the people make many pictures."

"But how do the people remember so many pictures?" Ahyoka asked. "Especially when they do not look like pictures."

Sequoyah shook his head. "I do not know."

They listened to utsonati, the rattlesnake, and tallalla, the woodpecker. When gugue, the quail, burst into flight, they drew her picture. When waya howled, they sketched the wolf. By sunlight, moonlight, and fire-light they drew picture after picture. By the middle of the summer the new stack reached Ahyoka's chin.

Ahyoka thought about her mother every day. She wondered whether Utiya had gathered many plants for trading or had finished many moccasins. Ahyoka watched the trail for her, but knew she must be taking another path through the Alabama forest to get to Willstown.

One morning Sequoyah said, "Today we will go to Willstown. We can trade the sassafras roots you gathered for the fishhooks we need."

"Could we see Tsiya?" asked Ahyoka. "I want to find out about Mother."

"Yes, Ahyoka. I wonder about Utiya too."

Sequoyah traded with Mr. Adair while Ahyoka walked to her aunt's cabin. She wondered why the women turned away from her as she passed. It puzzled her that the young children stopped playing and rudely stared at her. But she smiled when she saw Tsiya at her door.

"Go away, Ahyoka." Tsiya spoke before Ahyoka could even greet her. "You are no longer welcome here."

The smile left Ahyoka's face. All Tsalagi welcomed one another into their homes.

"But why?" she asked.

"Because your father makes evil. His magic killed Sali's cow. His magic made Wesa sick. Didanvwisgi, the Medicine Man, calls for revenge."

"You are wrong. My father works only on talking leaves, and they are not evil or magical," Ahyoka argued. "And I help him."

"Then, you are evil too," said Tsiya, shutting her door.

Ahyoka fought her tears. But they rolled down her cheeks anyway. Her father was not evil. He did not make magic. He only tried to understand the talking leaves.

"Ahyoka, what is wrong?" Sequoyah asked when her saw her tear-stained face.

"Why don't our people like us?" she asked.

"They are afraid of us because they do not understand what we are doing," answered her father.

"But when will they understand!" cried Ahyoka.

"When we can explain the talking leaves. You must be patient, Ahyoka. Many moons may pass before we find the answer." ·

"I want it to be now! We have worked so hard. Maybe we will never know the secret. Maybe the Adanvdo does not want us to read!" She ran out of the village and up the trail. Sequoyah did not catch up to her until they had almost reached the cabin.

Swirls of smoke rose over the forest. Ahyoka and her father stared, then rushed forward. But they knew what the smoke meant. The Didanvwisgi had taken his revenge!

The heat burned Ahyoka's face. She moved toward the burning cabin, but her father stopped her. She shook his hand free.

"The book, Father. They burned our book!"

"We can save only ourselves, Ahyoka," Sequoyah said sternly. The look in his eyes and the harshness of his voice silenced her.

"Come, Ahyoka," said Sequoyah. "We will not stay where we are hated. We will follow Climbing Bear's footsteps to the west and cross the Big River, the one white men call the Mississippi. There, with other Real People, maybe we can draw our pictures in peace."

With one last glance toward her former home, Ahyoka followed her father.

SIX

Ahyoka looked across the Etowah to Willstown. How would she remember her village? Would she draw the Council House and its cluster of cabins and lodges? The dogs sunning themselves in the dusty paths? Tsiya's cabin, with the cooking kettle outside? Her father handing her the book for the first time?

Ahyoka looked back up the trail. She imagined writing her mother a letter. She imagined her reading it and crying for her lost daughter. Would she then understand what they had been trying to do?

This time Sequoyah did not cross the ford to Willstown. Instead, he followed an old buffalo trail that led west and crossed the river farther on. He and Ahyoka picked persimmons and blackberries when they were hungry. They sipped cool spring water when they were thirsty. Ahyoka ached to ask how long it would take to get to the Big River. She wanted to know what they would eat and where they would sleep. But the distant look on her father's face told her to hold her questions inside.

As the sun dropped behind the mountains, they stopped for the night. Sequoyah chose a cave for shelter. He went to gather firewood while Ahyoka dug in the soft mud of the riverbank for worms. She had found five by the time her father returned. She took a hook. It looked just like one of the marks in the book, J. She poked the hook through a wiggling worm and, using a grapevine for a line, dropped it in the water.

As she fished, Ahyoka thought about what might happen now. She had never gone beyond Willstown. How far would they have to go to find other members of their tribe? Would Mother know she had left the

Big Mountains? If she and her father found other Real People, would they understand the search for the secret of the talking leaves, or would they shun them too? Maybe she could ask her father tonight.

Suddenly her line jerked. A fish! Ahyoka yanked on the vine and felt the fish take the hook. She pulled one way, then the other, as the fish fought to get loose. She felt her father come up behind her, and she expected him to take the line from her hands. But he didn't. At last the fish tired and Ahyoka flipped it up onshore.

Sequoyah grabbed the flopping fish and hit it with a rock. Then he looked at Ahyoka and smiled. "I do not think we have to worry as long as there are fish to catch and berries to pick."

After they had eaten, Sequoyah cut pine boughs for their beds. Ahyoka wished she had blankets, but they too had been destroyed in the fire. She moved Sequoyah's walking stick, flicking it in the sand. She smiled. Her scratchings looked like the tracks of knasgowa, the heron.

Darkness settled around them. Sequoyah's pipe glowed, small before the dancing circle of firelight. Smaller still, scattered across the sky, a sprinkling of stars winked at Ahyoka. She listened to the whispering of the river. Sequoyah sighed and lay back on the boughs. His deep, even breaths soon told her that he slept.

Ahyoka stayed awake. She put more wood on the fire until it burned crisp and bright. The flames leapt in lines and curves. When, at last, she fell asleep, Ahyoka dreamed of circles and lines. Swirling flames, curved fishhooks, and pointed heron toes filled her head.

Ahyoka woke before Sequoyah. She took his stick and stirred the fire. Sparks shot up from the coals sleeping under a log. The tip of the stick caught fire. Ahyoka pulled it across the sand to put out the flame. She had made a straight line. She dragged the stick again, adding a circle to the line.

First a line. Then a circle touching the line. Over and over she drew the same pattern. She could make the shapes from the book, but they meant nothing to her. She felt like one of the circles, having no beginning and no ending, going around and around, going nowhere.

The days turned to weeks as Ahyoka and Sequoyah traveled west. Sometimes they followed roads etched into the ground by white pioneers' wagons. At other times they traveled the trails made by deer or buffalo. They did not draw new pictures, but talked about the ones they had drawn before.

One morning the croaks of walosi, frogs, woke Ahyoka. She listened to them, wondering what they were saying to one another. She thought about the sounds other animals made. Uglu's hoot. Waya's howl. Gvna's gobble. Inadv's hiss. Many animals shared the same sounds. What if she and Sequoyah made pictures for each *sound* instead of for words and ideas? Then the same pictures could be used over and over, every time their sounds appeared in a word.

Sequoyah's eyes brightened for the first time in weeks when she told him her idea. "The animals share some sounds, just as

50

many Tsalagi words share sounds," she said.

Sequoyah looked at Ahyoka for a long time. Then he smiled. "Ahyoka, Sequoyah," he said. "Our names share sounds. Other words do too. Gadu and duya, bread and bean. Tsula and guwa, fox and mulberry. The same sounds are repeated. Let us say all the words we know and see if we hear the same sounds."

As they walked along, they called out the name of whatever they saw. Edoya, father. Ageyutsa, girl. Atsadi, fish. Tlugvi, tree. Gvna, turkey. Sedi, walnut. Ama, water. Ganvsge, leg. Ahawi, deer. They laughed every time two words contained the same sounds.

That night Sequoyah said, "Now we must draw a picture for every Tsalagi sound."

"But, Father, white men do not have a picture for each sound. In the book, I counted only as many shapes as there are fingers on five hands plus one finger more. They make more sounds than that. I have heard them speaking their own language."

Sequoyah was silent for a long time, then

said, "But each of the marks of the white man's talking leaves *must* show a sound he makes. By looking at the marks, he must know what sounds to make. And so, he sees the sounds of his words." Sequoyah suddenly stood up. He grabbed his walking stick and began drawing the white men's shapes in the dirt. Ahyoka joined him. They drew the shape of every mark they could remember.

"But what sounds do they make?" she asked.

"We do not care. Your name has three sounds. Ah-yo-ka. We will make this shape mean *ah*." He drew a D. "This can mean *yo*," and he drew h. "And this"—he drew e—"we will make say *ka*. Ahyoka."

Ahyoka copied the letters and said her name, "Ah-yo-ka."

"I think, my persistent little dosaudvna, you have found the secret of the talking leaves."

"No, Father," she said. "We found the secret together. And together we will make leaves that speak Tsalagi."

EPILOGUE

Many of the details of Sequoyah's life and his creation of the Cherokee alphabet were never recorded, but the outline of his efforts is known. This guided us as we wrote this book.

Sequoyah apparently became interested in "talking leaves" before or during his army service in the War of 1812. He realized the value of having a Cherokee alphabet to help the tribe in their treaty transactions with the United States government. Sequoyah was an accomplished silversmith, and used his artistic talents to draw the many pictures he first used as he began his search for the secret to the talking leaves.

Many Cherokees, however, felt he was practicing magic. His wife destroyed his bark pictures; later his cabin was burned. Willstown was probably on the Etowah River, in northeastern Alabama.

In 1818 Sequoyah went west to join other members of the Cherokee tribe already across the Mississippi River. By 1821, after about twelve years of determined work, he had perfected his syllabary, or syllable alphabet, of eighty-six symbols. Each letter represents a sound in Cherokee. Many of the symbols he chose came from the English alphabet, probably from books or newspapers he had seen. He used the letters right side up, upside down, and sideways. He changed some letters into different shapes and invented new ones.

At first the Cherokees were reluctant to learn Sequoyah's syllabic alphabet. One story tells how, in a test before the Cherokee Tribal Council, Ahyoka proved that she could read her father's talking leaves. Once they became convinced that the alphabet was not magical, the now-eager Cherokees practiced their writing on rocks, fence posts, and even on the inside walls of their homes. Within a year the majority of Cherokees were reading and writing in their own language.

The Cherokee talking leaves were so successful that in 1825 the New Testament was printed in Cherokee and in 1828 *Tsalagi Tsulehisanuinhi, The Cherokee Phoenix* newspaper, was first published.

Sequoyah became famous throughout the United States and Europe because he had accomplished something no one person had ever done before—he had created a written language from a spoken language. All other alphabets have been developed over long periods of time and by many people. In recognition for his efforts, the Cherokee people awarded him $500 a year and a silver medal inscribed in Cherokee and English on the front and with his picture on the back. Sequoyah proudly wore the medal for the rest of his life.

Sequoyah died in 1843 in Mexico in an attempt to find a "lost" tribe of Cherokees.

His burial place remains a mystery. But his genius is not forgotten. His statue stands in the Capitol in Washington, D.C. The state of Oklahoma, home to many Cherokees, was almost named Sequoyah. In 1849 the towering majestic redwoods were named sequoias in his honor and in 1890 Sequoia National Park was created. The Sequoyah Children's Book Award, honoring Sequoyah and supported by the Cherokee Tribal Council of Oklahoma and the Oklahoma Library Association, is given by the children of Oklahoma each year to their favorite book.

Our inspiration for this book comes from the following quote by Samuel Lorenzo Knapp, who met Sequoyah in Washington in 1828 and talked with him through translators (Sequoyah never learned English):

"By the aid of his daughter, who seemed to enter into the genius of his labors, he reduced them [the characters of his alphabet] at last, to eighty-six, the number he now uses."

History has, however, recorded even

fewer details of Ahyoka's story than Sequoyah's. She apparently did play an important role in helping her father unlock the secret of the talking leaves. What we have written is based on our knowledge of the Cherokee people of that time and of Sequoyah's own story. This book of fiction is anchored in that history. The Cherokee words, the customs, and the characters of Sequoyah and Ahyoka are based on our research. We hope that by telling this story of Ahyoka, we can help assure that her place in American history will be remembered.

Research for the book was conducted at the Cherokee National Museum and the Tsa-La-Gi Ancient Village, both operated by the Cherokee Nation. Additional research was done at Sequoyah's Home, operated by the Oklahoma Historical Society and the University of Oklahoma–Stillwater.

BIBLIOGRAPHY

Bird, Traveller. *Tell Them They Lie: The Sequoyah Myth*. Los Angeles: Westerlore, 1971.

Bleeker, Sonia. *The Cherokee*. New York: William Morrow & Co., 1952.

Carter, Samuel, III. *Cherokee Sunset: A Nation Betrayed*. New York: Doubleday, 1976.

Chiltoskey, Mary Ulmer. *Cherokee Words with Pictures*. Cherokee, N.C., 1972. (Self-published.)

Coblentz, Catherine. *Ah-yoka, Daughter of Sequoyah*. Evanston: Row Peterson & Co., 1950.

Coblentz, Catherine. *Sequoyah*. New York: Longmans, Green, and Co., 1946.

Foreman, Grant. *Sequoyah*. Civilization of the American Indian Series. Norman, Oklahoma: University of Oklahoma Press, 1987.

Forster, George. *Sequoyah, the American Cadmus.* Philadelphia: Office of the Indian Rights Association. Tahlequah, Cherokee Nation, 1885.

Mooney, James. *Myths of the Cherokee.* Washington, D.C.: Bureau of American Ethnology, Nineteenth Annual Report, 1897–98.

Mooney, James. *Historical Sketch of the Cherokee.* Chicago: Smithsonian Institution Press, Aldine Publishing, 1975.

Phillips, W. A. "Sequoyah." *Harper's New Monthly Magazine.* Volume XLI, 1870.

Roper, William. *Sequoyah and His Miracle.* Indian Culture Series. Billings, Montana: Indian Publications, 1972.

Woodward, Grace. *The Cherokees.* Civilization of the American Indian Series. Norman, Oklahoma: University of Oklahoma Press, 1979.